MW00879306

Overcoming the Battles Within:

A Love Triangle

By: NgoziChukwu O. Kemp

Table of Contents

Dedication

I dedicate this book to my loving husband, Eric, and to my daughters, Mary. Adrianna, Jasmine Kemp & Mel Blevins. Our animal family: Picachu, Shippo,& Cleo. Without my family, I would not have the courage to write this book. Most of all, I recognize God who is the greatest of all. Without him, I could do nothing.

Chapter 1

The Great Escape

Pam and Denise waited until Chukwuka left the house to go to work. As Chukwuka drove off, Pam and Denise grabbed Nneka and gathered their packed belongings, quickly leaving the house. It was a cold winter day, and Nneka complained about how cold it was. She didn't understand that she was leaving her father for good. Denise attempted to comfort Nneka, but she refused to hear anything she had to say. All Nneka wanted was her father. Pam was busy getting the bus arrangements to Georgia. "Honey, it's going to be alright. When we get to Georgia, you'll see Big Ma, Big Pa, and Granny." Pam would tell her daughter. Pam feared Chukwuka and what he would do if he got his hands on her. Pam whispered to Denise, who finally calmed Nneka down, "Chukwuka will never have the opportunity to send Nneka to Nigeria for good without me."

"That's my only child." Denise asked Pam, "What are you going to tell Ma and Pa about your marriage to Chukwuka? Is it truly over?" Pam replied to her sister, "Yes. Paul sent us enough money to catch the bus back to Georgia, and we can stay with Nathan and his family until we can get on our feet. Without our family's help, I don't know what Chukwuka would do to me. He's not going to realize that I filed for divorce and left until he gets home." Denise asked, "Are you sure we are doing the right thing? I mean, Chuks has the right to see his daughter. And are you sure old man Harris can be trusted?" Pam replied, "Old man Harris knows everything. He is a wise man, and he said he saw Chuks in a dream, sending Nneka back to Africa with him.

I would never see her again." Denise stated, "I hope you know what you are doing. Nneka may never forgive you for it. When Chukwuka arrives home from work, he walks into the gloomy house. He hears no sounds of laughter in the empty structure. All he sees are empty spaces that used to occupy the items of his wife and daughter. He came across a note that Pam left telling him that she and Nneka had left him for good. Chukwuka felt distraught. "How could she do this to me?" he thought "I thought things were getting better. I know things were not always easy, but we were going to have everything that we could ever imagine. What's going on? Why did you leave me in this empty house alone without my daughter?" All Chukwuka could think about was why did Pam do this to him. After he took a deep breath, his demeanor turned into rage against his wife. He began calling all his friends inquiring about the whereabouts of Pam and Nneka, but no one knew where they were. He called the police to start an investigation into Pam's whereabouts. Chukwuka began drinking several bottles of Star Lager and became violent. He threw several punches into the wooden doors causing several holes in the doors. He started throwing everything that he could find, including vases, his television set, and furniture, across the living room. Everything he did only made him think about what Pam did to him the most. "All I want is my daughter back." He yelled out. "Why did you take her? Why!" he screamed. When he finally calmed down, he called his family back home in Nigeria to tell his family what Pam had done. Nothing that his family said could relieve him from his heartbreak. As he sat in the lifeless home, he thought about good old Sandra, a friend he had at work. He called her and invited her to his home. Sandra had always wanted him. She disliked Pam with a passion because she wanted Chuks for herself. When Chukwuka confided in all his concerns, she only had her agenda in mind. "Pam is so selfish? Why did she do this to you? I told you she was no good for you. She doesn't deserve you." "You don't understand, Sandra; I still love my wife. She has Nneka with her. That was my world," Chukwuka exclaimed. Sandra had to think fast. She couldn't let that tramp spoil her opportunity. Suddenly, Sandra kissed Chukwuka hard and passionately, thrusting her tongue into his mouth.

Sandra began touching Chuks in areas that he had longed Pam to touch him in. "What are you doing?" Chukwuka asked. "I want you to relax and just go with the flow. Pam is not here. It is just me and you. I want you, and I want you badly." Sandra said. Chukwuka could feel the heat between him and Sandra. He glared into Sandra's piercing eyes and lost himself in them. "Yeah, I want you too," Chukwuka replied. He began caressing her breasts, kissing them ever so lightly. Sandra thrust her pelvis against his pelvis and continued to kiss him with extreme passion and intensity. Sandra proceeded down his stomach down against his pelvis. When she stopped at his member, she moved her tongue into the area that seemed forbidden with Pam. Chukwuka grabbed her hair and began to moan. Afterward, Sandra stopped and approached his bed. "Come get it. You know you want it". Chukwuka lost his cool, and they both plunged into the bed and slept together.

"I want my dad. Where is my dad? I want my dad." Nneka replied as tears went stream down her face. Pam tried to keep Nneka quiet, but Nneka cried out the most. "Maybe you want to tell the child the truth. She has the right to at least know that you guys are no longer a family." Denise replied. "Stay out of my business, Denise! I know what's best for Nneka. She is my daughter, not yours!" Pam retorted." "Pam, I just want to get back to Georgia. The sooner we get there, the better. I can't believe you got me caught up in your messy triangle." Denise said, looking out the window viewing the scenery. "If you are wrong about Chukwuka, you are going to regret what you have done. No matter what disagreements you have, he is still Nneka's father. He has rights, too," Denise proclaimed. "Stay out of my affairs and worry about yourself. You don't know what it is like to have children. This is my child!" Pam responded. "Just because I lost my baby doesn't mean I don't know what it is like, Pam. I think when Nneka gets older, she is going to know just what kind of person you really are, and you will be all alone. You have changed. Chukwuka deserves better. I just hate Nneka is in the crossfire. You can't separate their father-daughter bond." Pam stated, "I am going to make sure Chukwuka pays for everything he has done to me. I'm sure Sandra and Chuks are together right now as we are speaking. I am no longer there. She despised me and Chuks never could see it. It was always Sandra this or Sandra that. Now they can be happy. Nneka is my ticket out of this situation, and I am going to use it."

Chapter 2

Georgia Bound

After several days riding the bus, Pam, Denise, and Nneka final arrived at the bus station in Milledgeville, Georgia. The ride from Detroit was exhausting. Big Pa was waiting for us at his car. "Hello pumpkin. How are you? Big Pa is glad to see you, Nneka. How are you, Pam and Denise? Are you ready to go home?" "Yes, Big Pa, Big Pa, I miss my daddy. Is my daddy coming?" Big Pa looked at Pam and Denise, who then looked at each other. "Pam, what did you tell Nneka? You know she understands more than you think. She is five years old. She deserves to know why?" Big Pa stated. "Not you, too, Daddy. I had to hear all this coming from Denise all the way down from Detroit." "You left a good life and a good career with Chukwuka just to come back home. Is there something you are not telling me?" "No, Daddy, there is nothing you don't know. He's old news." Pam replied. "I hope you understand the consequences of quick decisions. It's harder to find a job down here than it was up North. Who are you staying with?" Big Pa responded. "We are staying with Nathan and his family. He said he didn't mind," Pam stated. "Alright, but you know Tiffany does not want you there. Nathan said he and Tiffany argued every day since the time he spoke to you because he didn't include her in making the decisions about your living arrangements." "What are you going to do for money? Did you think this plan went through?" Big Pa stated. Pam replied, "I sent all my money to Marilyn and Carlos to put into a bank account for me." "Your sister said Carlos was spending all the money you sent to put into a savings account. Carlos felt he was entitled to it since he is married to Marilyn. What are you going to do, Pam? Just think about it. Your momma and granny will be happy to see you." Big Pa responded.

Tiffany was sitting on the sofa smoking a cigarette. "Nathan. You didn't discuss with me the terms on which your sisters and their children will be staying here. You know Trisha needs her own privacy. We don't need this. You know Pam and I don't get along. I can tolerate Denise. You should have talked to me before you told them they could stay." Tiffany replied. "Tiffany, you know Pam has had a lot of problems in her marriage to Chukwuka. She had to get away from him. He would have sent my niece overseas to Nigeria. I didn't want that to happen. At least Paul sent her the money to come back home to Georgia. You know, Old Man Harris was right about Chukwuka." Nathan responded. "Forget about Old Man Harris!! That washed-up root, working drug dealer would say anything to get your money. What was in it for him? Huh? The pussy or the money? Why does Denise tag around Pam all the time? She acts like she doesn't have a life of her own. All your sisters and brothers act like because she is the oldest, you must cater to her. That is what she wants. She just wants to interfere with our marriage because hers is washed up. If she does not come to my face for anything, she will be alright. I don't trust Pam ever since she accused me of working that witchcraft stuff. She better watch out for Old Man Harris!! Why did you take her to him, anyway?" "Hell, that may be how Chukwuka got her." Tiffany retorted. "You got beef with all my family, and you think your family is better than mine. I wish you would try to get along with my sister. She is going through a tough time." Nathan responded. "And……, that's your sister. She is my sister-in-law. There is a difference." Tiffany responded.

Chapter 3

Meeting the Family

"Hello Big Ma, Hello Granny! I missed you! Big Pa bought me some ice cream! Is my daddy coming with us?" Nneka asked. Everyone was amazed with the question Nneka asked. It was silent. Nothing but a sigh came from Big Ma's mouth. "Your mama didn't tell you when your daddy was coming here?" she questioned. "Nneka, go outside and play with your other cousins. I'll call you inside when it's time to leave here and go to your Uncle Nathan's house." Pam answered. "You still didn't answer the question about Chuks. What's going on around here, and what are you not telling Nneka? You know that's Chuk's child, too." Big Ma responded. "Mama (sigh), I left Chuks for good. We have been having problems, and I felt that he was seeing other women. I tried talking it over with him, but he would always deny it. He was always calling other women, claiming they were friends. I didn't know if I could trust him." Pam said. "Did you try everything you could to work on your marriage? I don't think Chuks was the only problem. I think some of the problems came from you, too. You didn't try to work on your marriage. Why?" Granny asked. "Old Man Harris told me that he dreamed that Chuks was trying to take Nneka to Nigeria for good. I would never see her again." "Um mph, child, you should not be messing around that old root worker. You know he dibbles in that stuff. He isn't the right child. He might be trying to put a hex on you. Nathan was wrong for taking you there." Granny said. "You know Nathan and Denise tried to get your father to go to see him. He did, but that man tried to turn him against me. Told him I was trying to poison him. He said I was putting stuff on the ground and concrete to harm him. But your father refused to listen to him. He didn't go back to him anymore. That man had no control over your daddy. You might be making a mistake about Chukwuka. All the times he came down from Detroit to visit the family with you, all I could see is the love and respect he had for you. Yeah, there may have been women who tried to go after him but the thing that was standing in the way was you. He wasn't perfect, but he loved you. Now, you gave the other women the power to get him. That's just what Old Man Harris and those other women wanted, to break up your home." Big Ma replied. "Mama, why didn't you tell me?" Pam stated. "Because Pam, you are too headstrong and hard-headed. You would not have listened to me. You know how the old saying goes: misery loves company." Big Ma said. "Now you got to start all back over. You were a successful therapist in Detroit. Chuks held good jobs as an accountant. You guys had it all and now it's gone just like that. How are you going to provide for you and your child?" Big Pa asked. "And how come Marilyn don't help you out since Carlos almost spent your money?" Pam broke down and cried. "I......I don't know what to do. I'm scared. I thought I was doing the right thing. I used to be on top of the world. Now, I have nothing but me and my daughter. Chukwuka is going to pay!!" Pam yelled out. "Have you listened to anything we told you? Chukwuka is not entirely the problem. You sure got a lot to learn." Big Ma replied. Nathan drives into his parent's driveway. He gets out of the SUV and greets everyone. "Hey, Big Sis and Denise, how are you doing?" Nathan walks over to Big Ma and Granny, giving them a big hug. "Are you ready to go? Where's my niece?" he asked. "Playing under the shade tree, playing with Junior and Stacy. Where's Trisha? Are you ever going to bring her around?" Big Ma asked. "Mama, you know Tiffany. She's always finding something for that child to do." Nathan commented. "Son, I know Tiffany doesn't really care for this family. However, I do expect to see Trisha sometimes. You understand me, or else I'll get Tiffany told myself." Big Ma responded. "OK, Ma. I don't want World War III to start. I'll bring Trisha over when I come, I promise. When you guys are going to have more children? You know Trisha needs a playmate." Big Ma continued. "That will come in time. Right now, Tiffany and I are trying to get our stuff together." He replied as he continued to go to where Big Pa was outside. "I'll be ready to go when I finish talking to Daddy." "OK then. Let me load up our things into your SUV." Pam said.

Big Pa and Big Ma had 10 children. All the children came from all over. Pam was the oldest child. When she attended school in Sparta, her teachers didn't expect her to be successful. Her parents did not have time to help her with her studies because they were too busy working and raising her siblings. Children used to be mean and cruel. These kids would try to start fights with her, Marilyn, and Nathan a lot. Pam didn't go on many dates, and when she did date, the boy had to meet her father. Big Pa was a strong, stern man. Whatever he said, it went. There was no arguing about it. He didn't take any foolishness. If Big Pa said, "Be back home at 10 pm," you better be there at 9:45 pm. Any time later than 10 pm meant you were in serious trouble. Pam felt all alone and trapped. Her teachers felt that she was "slow." She only wished she could move out and get a job, but her dad insisted that she get a high school diploma. Both her father and mother didn't reach 12th-grade education. Big Ma was a housewife. She cooked, cleaned, and raised children. Big Pa worked for a brick-yard company. He made decent money, but every weekend, he would drink heavily. A lot of people didn't like Big Pa when he drank because he would become abusive and violent. Everyone had better stay out of his way. Big Ma would take her children over to Granny's house many nights to keep Big Pa, the mighty Henry Ray Cummings, from hurting them. However, over the years, he changed from his violent ways to learning about Jesus. When Big Pa changed, he learned to read his bible. He became a good father to his wife and children. Pam wasn't fortunate to see the change since she moved away from home during her teenage years.

When school let out for the Summer, Uncle Duke (Big Pa's brother) came down all the way from Niagara Falls, New York. He was on a mission. He came to rescue Pam from her misery. He offered Pam the chance to live with him and his family while attending college. That was Pam's dream and her ticket out of Sparta. She couldn't pass this chance up. Carlos had his eye on Pam for a long time. However, after Pam left, he married Marilyn. They had 5 children together.

Carlos was in between jobs (not keeping a steady job). When he got paid, he blew his money on alcohol. Carlos was a bad alcoholic and didn't do much to provide for his family. Marilyn was left to provide for the family. Marilyn took odd jobs to make ends meet. Marilyn continued to work this way until she decided to go to school to become a licensed practical nurse. With a lot of hard work, Marilyn paid her way through school and passed the state boards to become a nurse. Marilyn and Carlos had an estranged relationship. Sometimes, they couldn't stand to be around each other. Marilyn worked hard to provide for the family, but Carlos was never home. He would hang out with his boys and run around with other women. When he got home after doing his thing, he would come home to be abusive to Marilyn. "Where you been! YOU didn't have my food ready! What am I supposed to eat?" Carlos shouted. "Will you lower your voice? You are going to wake up the children. You know I was at work, and I didn't have time to cook dinner, besides, where have you been?" Marilyn replied. "Woman, you don't ask me about where I been! I am the man of this house!" Carlos retorted. "You think you are the man everywhere else except with your family. You can barely keep a job, you don't spend time with your children, but you have time for everything and everybody else." Marilyn answered back. Suddenly,

Carlos punched Marilyn in the face. "You don't tell me what to do or how to run things around here! I am in charge!" Carlos responded. Marilyn grew silent and walked away from him. Marilyn was bleeding out from her mouth. A couple of teeth were knocked out of place. Carlos continued to harass Marilyn, but she ignored him as if he wasn't there. In her eyes, he was disgusting to her. Such disgrace fell upon her face as she walked away from him. "Let this be your last time hitting me, or else," Marilyn answered. "What are you going to do to me? Call the cops? I will be right back out. Then what?? You get your ass kicked again or worse than the first time?? You are mine! This family is mine! You are not going anywhere!" Carlos responded loudly. Emma (the middle child) came downstairs and saw her mother with her face swollen. "Mama, what happened?" she exclaimed. "Baby, go back upstairs, I'm ok. Go on now, child." Marilyn answered. "Your daddy is just a little angry". Emma wanted to ask more questions, but Marilyn rushed Emma upstairs to protect her from Carlos. "Take that little whore upstairs before she sees what I'll do to you," Carlos said. "You will not lay a hand on my child. I will see to that." Marilyn stated. Carlos suddenly began throwing up all over the floor and passed out on the sofa. He was out for the night.

Chapter 4

Niagara Falls

Pam attended Central University in Niagara Falls, New York. She stayed with her Uncle Duke and Aunt Thelma until she moved out. She was able to get an apartment of her own. Uncle Duke adored Pam being, his eldest niece. Aunt Thelma, on the other hand, had an issue with Pam being there. There was always a complaint about Pam. "Duke, she is lazy. She won't clean up after herself. What kind of man is going to want her." she replied. "My niece is welcomed in this home. Don't you see. I am trying to help her? Sparta is not the place for her to be right now. She got potential. I can see it in her." Uncle Duke responded. The arguments, however, continued until one day, her father sent her a letter with enough money to get an apartment of her own. "Pamela, you got to get a job and use whatever money you have to keep your apartment. Your daddy wanted to make sure you had what you needed." Uncle Duke replied. "I am sorry, Uncle Duke. I seem to cause trouble everywhere I go. I don't belong nowhere." Pam responded.

"I love you, Pamela Mae. You have made me very proud of you. You are in school, and you are about to graduate. You are an adult now. You can make it. You have got to make it. So many people are against you. Remember, darling, I believe in you, and so does your family back home." Uncle Duke replied. This would be the last time Pam would see Uncle Duke alive. After Pam moved out, Uncle Duke had a heart attack while he was sleeping. Pam was weak and distraught. She couldn't bear to go to the funeral. All Pam wanted to do was to curl up and disappear.

"Pam, don't let those strange men come up to your apartment. Those men don't want nothing but one thing, and they will bout do anything to get it." Pam remembered Big Pa saying before she left for Niagara Falls. Pam finally got a roommate named Velvet, who also attended Central University. The two became best friends. Velvet and Pam worked together at "Tippy's Coffee Shop." Pam and Velvet shared some of the same classes together. Velvet was majoring in Social Work whereas Pam was majoring in Counseling and Therapy. They were joined to the hip. They were study partners who were always challenging each other to do better. During the Summer of 1970, both Pam and Velvet were set to graduate. They completed all their requirements and were excited about finally being done with college. They could use a break. "Who is coming to your graduation, Pam?" Velvet asked. "Nobody. Daddy couldn't take time off from the brickyard. Mama just had another child. My Uncle Duke gone, and I feel so all alone." Pam responded. "My dad is traveling to California to close some big deal for the company he works for. How about we invite some guys over just for some company." Velvet replied. "I-I-I-I-I don't know about that. I mean, my daddy told me not to invite boys over. They only want one thing." Pam said nervously. "Come on Pam, you aren't in the country no more. You are in Niagara Falls. You are grown now. If you don't give up anything, you are fine. Stop being so scared. Grow up!" "Velvet, I guess you are right. If Daddy don't find out about it, I'm fine."

Chukwuka and Roberto knocked on the door. "Who is it?" Velvet asked. "It's Chuks and Rob," Rob shouted out. "You invited us here, remember?" "Yeah, Yeah, I'm coming to the door. Just give me a few minutes," Velvet yelled back. "Pam, will you go answer the door for me? I'm still getting ready." "Okay," Pam replied. Pam opened the door, and she could not believe what she saw. She saw two very handsome young men. Chuks had a milk chocolate complexion with brown eyes and a medium body frame. Just by looking at his build, he looked very athletic. He had the most dazzling smile, which left you speechless. He had white teeth, which could be compared to porcelain. Everything about him was beautiful. Chuks and Pam locked eyes at their first meeting. Pam was intrigued with Chuks, but she didn't want anyone to know how much she really liked him. Chuks was attracted to Pam and gave a dashing smile of confidence when they met. Roberto was Velvet's type. He was a shade darker than Chuks but was very cocky about his looks. Roberto was slightly taller than Chuks and also had an athletic body frame. Roberto had silky, shiny hair that was flowing in the sun. Rob had clear blue eyes that appeared as if they could see into your inner soul.

When Velvet arrived at the door, she saw how Pam was acting and tried to get the obvious attention off Pam. "Would you guys like to come in?" The guys looked at each other and then said, "Sure, thanks." "Thanks, Velvet, for inviting us over. I am glad to get over finals. I am ready to graduate, but I need a little outlet," Rob stated. "Have you guys introduced yourselves to my roommate and friend Pam? She is from Georgia. She's studying Counseling and Therapy." Velvet replied, looking at Rob with intensity. "Hi Pam, I am Rob. I am a friend of Velvet's." Rob stated. "I am Chukwuka Okafor. I am from Nigeria originally. I am living with a cousin who is attending school here in Niagara Falls. I have gotten accepted into the School of Accounting at Central University. I am studying Accounting." Pam was impressed. Chuks was a pick for any female. He was handsome, intellectual, and smart. He was someone my dad would be proud to have as a son-in-law. "I am thinking too far into the future. I don't know him or his family. I just know I want him." Pam thought.

After dinner, the gang decided to eat at a Mexican restaurant called "The Mexicana." It was the best restaurant to go to. The guys paid for the girls' meals, and then they headed to the movies.

The couple watched a scary movie called "The Abyss Within the Corn Fields." Whenever a scary scene came on, Rob would grab Velvet's hand tight and steer her close to him. Chuks would hold Pam tight and whisper softly in her ears, "Are you okay? You are not too scared, are you?" All Pam could think about was staying in his arms forever. She did not want to let him go.

After the movie was over, both couples returned to the apartment. Velvet stared into Rob's eyes. She wanted to invite him in for an overnight stay, but she knew Pam would not stand for that. Pam was a "good girl" and was afraid of what her father may say or do. "We will plan a date for just me and you. How does that sound?" Rob asked. "I think I like your style already. That will be just fine." Velvet stated. Little did Velvet know what Pam was really thinking. "Chuks, I enjoyed our date. I hope that we can get together again one day?" Pam commented.

"Pam, I want to see you again. I know that it has been a short time, but I like you a lot. I want to get to know you better. How about we go out next Saturday?" Chuks asked. "I would love to," Pam stated. Pam forgot all about being the country girl who came to New York from Georgia. Pam felt that, for the first time, she was an adult. She knew what she wanted. It didn't matter that Chuks was a foreigner. All she knew was that she liked him a lot. She felt as if it could possibly be a start to something beautiful.

Chapter 5

Marriage

"Pam, how does the dress fit? You know it must be just right for you to walk down the aisle." Velvet added. "It fits fine. You did a great job on it. I never thought this day would come," Pam said excitedly. "Pam, just make sure he treats you right. Guys can be tricky. They can be one way today and another on a different day. Some guys are not faithful. You are a nice girl, and you are pure. Some guys like to pursue it as a challenge. Not all guys are like that, but you only dealt with him. Take care of yourself." Velvet mentioned with concern. She was unusually concerned for her friend. "Velvet, is there something you are not telling me?" Pam asked. "No, no. Just never mind me. I am just overbearing," Velvet retorted. "Velvet, I know things have been tough for you, especially after the breakup with Rob. You have been through a lot. Don't worry. I will be fine. Daddy and Mama will be here. I think they really like him. I feel like the luckiest person in the world right now!" Pam exclaimed. "Ok, Pam, just as long as you know, I am here for you if you need me," Velvet replied. Velvet stepped away from Pam to keep her from seeing her cry. Pam was her best friend, but she didn't realize what she was getting into with Chuks. There were endless fights between herself and Rob pertaining to the way Chuks treats women. She wanted to tell her best friend the truth. But how could she spoil it on her big day?

Pam walked slowly down the aisle as her bridesmaids followed behind her. Her Matron of Honor was standing right there next to her being supportive of her best friend. Chuks walked down the aisle with confidence. His best man, Rob, was standing next to him. Velvet thought of what it would be like if Rob and herself were getting married. She soon brought herself back to the realization that things could never be the same again between Rob and herself. She knew that Rob will always support Chuks, even when he knew he was wrong. Chuks didn't care about the repercussions; all Chuks wanted was what he could get when he wanted it. The list went on from other women to permanent citizenship in the U.S. It didn't matter how, just if he could keep it from Pam (who didn't have a clue about Chuks dealings). Velvet felt like a traitor because she could not tell Pam about Chuks. She couldn't even tell Pam that she was pregnant and the father of her unborn child was Chuks. Not even Rob knows the truth. She couldn't hurt Pam.

The last thing that Velvet heard was Chuks telling Pam "I do" to the marriage vows that were exchanged. Velvet tried so hard to fight back her tears. "Once they are married, I can relocate. Chuks will never have the chance to catch up with me or be a part of this child's life." Velvet thought to herself. Velvet felt that what Pam will discover about Chuks will be the tip of the iceberg. Once the vows were exchanged and the couple became "man and wife," Chuks carried Pam over the threshold. The couple glared into one another's eyes and were passionately kissing each other (desiring to have a heated night of intimacy).

Pam's mother and father looking on proudly as their oldest daughter disappeared from their eyes and rode off into the sunset. If only they knew what the future held for their daughter couple finally arrived at a luxury hotel called "The Cove." Pam and Chuks couldn't keep their hands off each other. Pam finally broke the silence. "Chuks, I thought your family would be here so that I had the opportunity to meet them." "My father had a very important business meeting. He couldn't fly out here for the wedding. Mother wanted to come, but she had to take care of my siblings. They would love to meet you. One day, we can fly to Nigeria and meet them." Chuks replied. "I would love that very much," Pam stated as she undressed Chuks for the festivities. She was ready, and Chuks was anticipating the events to follow. "I want you, and I want you bad," Pam replied as she glared into Chuks eyes. Chuks began to guide her to the bed and started to kiss her passionately from her lips to her breasts and belly button. He went from there to the vagina, tickling her clitoris. All Pam could do was scream in excitement. And the night began.........

Chapter 6

Motherhood

Motherhood wasn't easy for Pam. Chuks was never home because he was working all the time. Pam and Nneka spent many days alone. Chuks worked late many nights. Whenever Pam wanted Chuks to show some affection, he was always tired. Pam started thinking, "Is this what marriage and being a mother is all about? I didn't sign up for this." Pam wanted her marriage to work, but she had some insecurities. Sandra, a woman that Chukwuka says is a co-worker, has been calling him regularly. Pam didn't like what she was feeling. Normally, Pam was not the jealous type. However, her intuition was on full alert. Pam didn't know what was going on between those two, but it had to stop.

Pam was breastfeeding Nneka as Chukwuka walked in from work. "Hi, honey. How was your day at work?" Pam asked. "Oh, Pam, it was so busy," Chukwuka stated. "We are receiving more new clients. The company has asked me to work overtime and some late nights because they say I am the best accountant they have. I know that the money would help us out and we wouldn't have to worry about anything. How has Nneka been feeling today?" Chukwuka responded. "Nneka is doing better. She is recovering well. I have been making sure that she takes her medications and that she is hydrated. Chuks, I need help with her. You work all the time. When do we have time for the both of us?" Chuks smiled. "I know that it is tough on you right now, but it will get better. I promise," he replied. "When Chuks, when? I am taking care of the house and Nneka. I don't talk much to my family or my friends. It's almost like I am alienated away from them. I haven't seen Velvet in years. My Big Pa and mom don't have the time to visit because they are either working or taking care of my siblings. I feel so all alone." Pam complained. "Why don't you become friends with Sandra, my coworker? She always asks about you. Maybe you two can go out and have lunch together or something." Chukwuka implied. "Chuks, I don't feel comfortable being around her. I have mixed feelings about her. I don't trust her. She calls you all the time like she does not have a husband already. I don't like it. Pam retorted. "Like I told you before, Pam. She is a coworker on my job. She has helped me out a lot on the job. That's all. You have to learn to trust me." Chuks replied. "I think she has the hots for you, Chuks. I don't like it." Pam responded back firmly. "Look, you can think what you want. I am going out." Chuks replied. He started to become angry with Pam, and her accusations did not help the situation. "Chuks, where are you going?" Pam asked. "Out! Do you understand!" Chuks raising his voice. "Chuks, every time I ask you something you don't like, you always have to go out and get a drink. Why won't you spend some quality time with me and your daughter? What have we done to you?" Pam asked painfully. "I don't have time for this. I am gone. I will see you when I come back." Chuks replied as he stormed out of the room. This was just the opportunity he needed to see Sandra. What happened between Chuks and Sandra wasn't supposed to happen, but he just couldn't keep his mind off her. Pam asked too many questions. How dare she ask me anything? She doesn't work. She takes care of the house and Nneka. "I love Pam, but she does not fulfill all my sexual needs. I just can't get enough of the sex the other women give me. I can't let Pam know, or she will leave me and take Nneka with her. I got to be a husband in the public and a freak at night." Chuks thought. "If she only knew... I just can't hurt her." "Maybe I should just go to see Sandra. I know how she feels about me. Maybe she can listen to me, and something more can develop from it."

Chapter 7

The Awakening

Pam was going through and cleaning up her bedroom. As she was cleaning out the drawers on Chuks' side of the bed, she ran across some condoms and a picture from Sandra. She also saw letters where Sandra and Chuks were corresponding. Pam remembered the telephone calls that Chuks would receive from her. He stated that they were "business calls" regarding the job. Everything within her wanted to read the letters. "I want to see if he is telling the truth," she thought. As she proceeded to read a letter that Sandra wrote, she noticed a picture of a little boy. She looked at the back of the picture. It had Velvet's signature on it. "Why would Velvet send Chuks a picture of her son and never think about writing her or even calling me? That's some strange shit." Pam thought. Again, Pam was about to read the letter when she heard the front door in the living room open. It was Chuks. Boy, he had some explaining to do. However, now is not the time. I have to get to the bottom of these mysteries. Pam's gut feelings tell her that Chuks is not as faithful as she thought he was. Sandra was a no-brainer, but who are the other women he is having sex with? "It surely isn't me. He is always so tired when he comes in from work. He didn't expect me to clean up his side of the room, and instead, I am going through his things." Pam thought. "Now is not the time to confront him. I have a lot of things to investigate. My husband is not loyal to me." Pam reasoned to herself. "Hello honey, how is your day going?" Chuks exclaimed as he was wondering why Pam looked so strange. "I sure hope she hasn't been going through my belongings."

Chuks thought. "Oh, I am fine. How was your day?" Pam asked as she had to pretend nothing was wrong. "I have great news! I got a raise and a promotion today. I am the senior accountant at the Carson, Norwood, and Blake firms. I am excited! This means we are getting closer to our dreams." Chuks exclaimed. Chukwuka's Nigerian accent was growing stronger and stronger as he made his announcement. "I am so proud of you, Chuks. We are on our way." Pam said as she tried to pretend she was excited. She had a lot on her mind about their marriage, and this news made things more difficult for her. "I am going down to make dinner. Congratulations again. I am truly happy for you." Pam said as she walked away. "Who is this promotion going to benefit anyway?" Pam thought.

Denise decided to call Pam since she hadn't heard from her in a while. Pam was glad to hear her voice. She felt isolated because Chuks didn't like her having many friends unless he approved of them. He didn't want any friction in his marriage, and he wanted to do what he wanted without any drama. "Hi, Denise. I am so glad to hear from you. What's on your mind?" Pam asked. "I just wanted to reach out to you and see how you and the family are doing. Your family in Georgia misses you." Denise stated. "I am fine, and we are fine. All is well. I am so glad to hear your voice." Pam retorted. "Is something wrong, Pam? You sound a little different from usual." Denise stated with concern. "I just got a lot of things going on, but I am okay," Pam replied. As Denise was about to conclude their conversation, she replied, "Okay, Pam, I am here when you want to talk. Do you understand?"

Chuks and Sandra locked their tongues together passionately while Chuks caressed Sandra's breasts. He proceeded down Sandra's breasts and was kissing her belly button. Sandra began to moan and groan as he was making her hotter and hotter. "I want you, Sandra," Chuks responded. "How do I know how you really feel about me instead of trying to get a booty call? I mean, Pam is your wife. I don't like her or the fact that you are married. What are you going to do if you want me?" Chuks began to wander and think. "This chic thinks I am going to leave Pam for her. I just want some play, and whatever I want, I get." Chuks thought to himself. "Just shut up and let me serve you," Chuks responded as he avoided her previous questions. After exploring her belly button, he went down to her vagina and started licking her clitoris. The more he kissed her clitoris, the more Sandra groaned, making her hotter and hotter. Chuks began to take his first two fingers and fondled her vagina, increasing her sensations until she would climax. Her knees were weak after he was done. "Chuks, I want you. When are we going to stop playing around? I mean, I want you bad. I just don't want to anticipate it; I want to get it on." Sandra said emotionally. She began to feel his big, beautiful brown dick begin to penetrate inside her vagina. That's what she wanted the whole time and all he does is tease her. "In due time, Sandra. In due time." I just want you to think of me the next time you are here."

Chuks replied.

Chapter 8

The Truth

It was Chuks and Pam's 5th wedding anniversary. Pam didn't have a clue about what Chuks was planning for her. She just knew she had mixed feelings about her marriage. All she wanted was for her husband to love her deeply. Pam always had intuitions that just did not add up. She wandered why some of the women that Chuks were in contact with would smirk or laugh or make faces when they saw her with him. Deep down, Pam had an uncanny feeling that things were not right and things weren't getting any better. Chuks was distant and spent more time at work than with his family. He also volunteered to work extra hours. "I love Chuks. Why is he treating me like this?" Pam questioned. "Does he really even love me in the first place?"

Although Chuks was having issues messing around with Pam, he truly loved her. In his mind, he had the best wife in the world and had a beautiful little girl. His marriage, however, needed some work. "The problem isn't Pam, it's me. I can't seem to control keeping my dick in my pants." he thought. "I want to make things right with Pam. She is sweet, loving and kind. She puts up with my baggage, and that's not fair to her, our marriage, or our family. I got to make things right with her, and I got to make a change before it's too late." Chuks decided to take Pam for a night out in town and for dinner. The ultimate gift I will give her is a vacation for both of us to Cancun, Mexico. We need this time to relax, get away from our problems, and reacquaint ourselves with each other. Nneka can stay with my friend

Jonathan and his wife Paulette while we are on vacation. This way, we can have some time to work out differences and make our marriage work. I got to work on me. I don't want to lose my family." Chuks reasoned. Chuks decided to leave the office early and surprise Pam. That way, she would know he was thinking of her.

Chuks entered the house cheerfully and jolly. "Pam, I am home." Pam looked surprised. "What! You are home early. I thought you had some things you had to finish up on at the office." Pam said while she was completing household chores. Chuks walked over to her and gave a lavish, long, heartfelt kiss. "Happy Anniversary, Baby! I love you!" Chuks exclaimed. "Oh honey, what has gotten into you? This is not like you at all," Pam said, looking shocked. "Baby, I am sorry for all the things I put you through and how I treated you. I had issues that only I could deal with. I love you and Nneka, and I think I should do better by you guys." Chuks reasoned. "I have a surprise for you. Get dressed, Pam. We are going out. Nneka can stay with Jonathan and his wife Paulette for a couple of days."

Chuks replied. Tears of joy started streaming down Pam's face. " I, I thought that you didn't love me, Chuks. I thought you were messing around with me. I love you, Chuks, and I want our marriage to work. I just don't understand you sometimes." Pam stated. Immediately, Chuks shut down anything else that Pam was about to say with a passionate kiss that lasted like an eternity, "Put on your

best attire and pack up some clothes. We are going off for a few days,"
Chuks said. Pam embraced Chuks with a warm, loving hug. "Thank
you, Chuks. I know without a doubt you love me. Please don't hurt
me." Pam pleaded. "I don't plan on it," Chuks confirmed. It was as if
Chuks had become a new man.

Chuks and Pam went on a night in the town. First, they
stopped to eat at a Mexican restaurant named "La Corizon." It was
one of the best restaurants in town. Chuks gazed into Pam's eyes as if
he had fallen back in love with her all over again. "I don't know why
I do what I do to her. She is the woman I love, but I constantly sleep
around. Things have got to change. Mom and Dad were right. I must
concentrate on my family." "Chuks, are you okay?" Pam asked,
breaking Chuks out of his thoughts. "Yeah, Pam. I am fine now."
Chuks replied.

Chuks cellphone began to ring. It was Velvet. "Pam, I got to take
this call. This is Sam from the office. I will be right back." Things
seemed to return right back to normal. Pam gave a look of disgust as
the moment between her and Chuks was beginning to fade away.
Chuks walked over toward the restaurant's water fountain. "Hello,
Velvet. I hope this is important. I was spending time with my wife."
Chuks commented in an annoying tone. "Since when did that stop you
from sexting me up? Tell my best friend I said hello. Why do you
keep me from speaking to her? Oh, because she will find out the truth

and history between me and you. Have you told your daughter about her brother Nicholas? He's been missing his daddy. He needs clothes shoes, and I need some new clothes and hair done along with my nails. I'm sure you can handle that; as a matter of fact, I know you can."

"Velvet, don't try to threaten me. You know it doesn't work like that. When I come to California to see Nick, I will give you some money. I am only coming to see Nick. You know me, and you are done. What has I am ever done to you for you to resent her the way you do? She used to be your best friend or bestie, as you call it." Chuks retorted. "When she married you and you didn't tell her about me or Nick for that matter. You are the one who is disgusting. The many days and nights Nick had to be home without his father. How terrible can you be? Pam is too trusting and naïve to think you really love her as many times as you have slept with me. My abortions tell the whole story, and yet you claim you love her so much. Just dirty." Velvet answered.

"You wish it was you, don't you? You wish I had married you. That's not how it works, sweetheart. I love Pam. I don't have to justify anything to you. I wouldn't marry you because you were so easy to get with. Everyone around the way got with you. You were trying to make Pam become you. You were jealous of her and tried to ruin her. Pam is the person I had my eyes on the whole time. You were just there for convenience. I love my son Nick. I am sorry he must endure this, and I am taking care of him, not you. Take care of my son. You better not have all those men over to the house or have him calling them "daddy," or else I will destroy you and your family. You know your dad owes me money, too. He failed you and Nick. I will gain custody of Nick, and you will have nothing left, not even me, to pick up the pieces. Now, back to my wife. Don't call me again unless it is an emergency about Nick." Chuks responded. "But...." Velvet attempted to respond, but Chuks had hung up on her. "Lazy bitch." He thought. When he walked back over to the table, Pam gave a repulsive look. "How long was you going to stay on the cellphone while I was sitting here? I thought this outing was about me and you." Pam retorted. "Baby, it was about some unfinished business. Look, we were having a wonderful time enjoying each other; don't spoil it." Chuks replied. "And I am sorry for leaving you here so long." "Apology accepted," Pam answered. "Now, let's order the food."

After the Pam and Chuks left the restaurant, the two went to the most expensive hotel in town. Pam looked on in awe and amazement. Chuks leads Pam to the most beautiful hotel room she has ever seen. "Chuks, how can you afford to take me out like this when you were so strict about our expenses at home? Will this set us back?" Pam asked. "With the promotion I received at my job, yes, we can afford it." "But Chuks," Pam tried to reason as Chuks thrust his tongue in her mouth, kissing Pam passionately. The kiss seemed like it was never going to end. "Oh, I love you, Chuks. I never felt the way you make me feel these past couple of days." Pam responded. "Thank you for everything." "You are welcome, darling. My pleasure."

Chuks commented. Chuks had his cell phone on vibrate so that Pam would not suspect anything. He wanted this night to be special.

Chuks wasn't going to let up until he was tired. All he wanted to do was please his wife at whatever the cost. They made love on and on into the morning. Chuks was pleased when he looked over at his wife to see she was exhausted from their lovemaking. He stroked her head for several minutes. His cell phone rang. This time, it was Sandra. "What are you doing? I am thinking about you. I want to have wild sex with you." Sandra continued but was interrupted by Chuks. "I am with my wife. Don't call me. I will call you if I need anything." Chuks replied. He didn't want to wake Pam up and start World War III.

"But Chuks, I…" Sandra tried to say her last couple of phrases before Chuks hung up his cell phone. "What's going on? Who was that?" Pam asked. "Just someone who had a wrong number," Chuks replied. "Oh, okay, let's go back to sleep," Pam stated. "Okay, my love," Chuks said as he turned over and hugged his wife. They slept into the morning.

Chapter 9

The Reckoning

The next day, Chuks made breakfast to Pam for the invigorating night they shared previously. When Chuks presented the breakfast tray to Pam, the tickets for their trip was lying beside the dish. "What is this in the envelope?" Pam asked. "It is our tickets to Cancun, Mexico. I thought that you would like them. I think that the vacation is much needed." Chuks commented. Pam leaped out of bed to hug Chuks. She had a smile on her face from ear to ear. "I love you so much! You have really changed. Whatever it is, I like it," Pam replied. "Anything to please the wife," Chuks commented. Chuks began to think about Sandra and how he treated her. "I got to get back in good with Sandra or she will never forgive me. She gives me what I want whenever I ask." Chuks thought. The old man in Chuks began to come back again.

The past few weeks had been rough on Pam. She has not been feeling quite like herself lately. Pam felt nauseated and vomited every time she ate something that did not agree with her. "What is going on with me? This is not like me feeling tired all the time," Pam thought. Pam decided to make an appointment with her physician to find out what was wrong with her. Her menstrual period had not been normal for about a month. Pam thought that she was done having children.

Pam finally made it to her check-up. After lab work and tests were run on her, the doctor came into the room with an excited look on her face. "According to the tests and lab work that were performed, you are pregnant. You said you haven't had a regular menstrual period in over a month. When was the last time you had sex with your husband?" Dr. Escovedo asked as. Pam remembered the very last time she had intercourse with Chuks. "It was approximately three weeks ago," Pam answered. "That may have been about the same time you got pregnant. Congratulations are in order," Dr. Escovedo replied. "This is a big surprise to me. I haven't had a regular period in a month. I thought childbearing for me was a thing of the past. I don't know what to think." Pam said. "You have time to decide what you want to do. It will be great if you gave Nneka a little sister or brother. If you don't want to have the baby, you have choices." Dr. Escovedo replied. "Thank you, Dr. Escovedo. I will keep you informed of what I will do." Pam commented.

Pam didn't know what to do. She was shocked and surprised at the same time. She wanted to tell Chuks the news, but something keeps her from thinking that right now is not the right time to tell him. There are several things that she needs to consider. Her situation with Chuks was not getting better. "These stressors could make me lose the baby," she thought. "I just need to relax and meditate on what my choices are."

Chuks was in a dilemma. "How did I get into this triangle?" he thought. "I love Pam, but I think about Velvet and Sandra constantly. Not to mention the other one-night stands that I may encounter. It would hurt me if I lost Pam, but I want the freedom to do what I want without answering anybody. I guess I don't know what I want," Chuks thought. "How will I handle this? I don't want Pam to leave because I love her and Nneka, but these feelings of lust I can't shake; I'm like a kid in a candy store." Chuks concluded.

Pam met Antoine at a grocery store. It was something about her. He just couldn't keep his eyes off her. He didn't know how to approach her for fear of getting rejected. He just had to speak to her anyway. "Hello, my name is Antoine," he announced. "Hello, I'm Pam," she replied. "I just couldn't help but notice how beautiful you are. I am not trying to give you a line, but you are just gorgeous. Does anyone ever tell you that?" he asked. Pam felt like a breath of fresh air had come in her direction. No, no one (not even Chuks) made her feel this special. It was amazing how a stranger can appreciate someone else's essence. "I don't usually get many compliments. I tend to stay to myself. I appreciate you taking an interest, though," Pam replied while walking off from Antoine. He could see the hurt and pain in her eyes. "Pam, I would like to get to know you better. I understand if you are married or have a significant other. I just want to get to know you better. I find your beauty remarkable. You seem to be a good person inside and out. Your man better appreciate what he has, or someone else may just come and sweep you off your feet. Here is my number: (878) 756-1298." Antoine commented. Pam's eyes brightened up so much as if she could see stars. No one seemed to take this much time to notice her. She was afraid to take his number; however, she thought what was wrong with having a friend of the opposite sex. Chuks does it all the time. It felt good feeling notice. "I am married; however, I like talking and meeting new people. I never knew that someone could ever brighten my day like you have in only a few minutes. You are not a con artist or felon, are you?" Pam asked. "Noo, I just like meeting beautiful women. I find you very interesting," he replied. "My number is (878) 239-1305. You can call me any time before 4:30 pm. That's when my husband comes home from work. I will inform you of other times when available." Pam commented. "Your husband better watch out," Antoine stated as he started walking away. "Not bad for a 35-year-old mother of 1 and ½. I am pregnant, and I didn't think anyone would ever notice me. It's time to heat this game up a notch." Pam thought.

Chapter 10

Fantasy vs Reality

It has been several weeks since Pam has been conversing with Antoine, and he has helped her to forget her troubles with Chuks, the other women, and her pregnancy. Pam did not even care about what was going on between her and Chuks. She looked forward to her talks with Antoine. He made her feel special, and the only one he was giving his attention to. Pam was careful not to speak on the issues she was having in her marriage or her pregnancy. All she wanted was to feel "good" about herself. "I don't want this feeling to ever come to an end," Pam thought to herself.

One day, Pam was completing chores around the house. She was not feeling her best, so she decided to sit down on the sofa. Pam noticed scant amounts of blood trickling down her thigh into her pantiliner. Pam started experiencing severe clotting as the clots may its way down her leg. Severe cramping followed. "This can't be," she thought. "Oh my God," Pam screamed out. "Chuks, help me! Please, someone please help me!" No one was home. Pam lowered herself down to the floor. She began to curl up into a circle and brawl. Pam knocked her cell phone down to the floor. As she reached towards her cell phone, Pam suddenly fell unconscious.

When Pam awakened, she noticed that she was in a hospital bed covered in a blanket. Chuks was sitting at her bedside, waiting for Pam to wake up. Nurse Chrissy came into the room. "Where am I?" Pam asked. "You are very lucky, you know that." the nurse said as she was flushing Pam's IV line. Your husband found you unconscious, lying on the floor. You are at General Memorial Hospital. You seemed to be asking for Antoine. I guess that was your brother, huh? It's good to have a good bond like that." the nurse mentioned. "You almost didn't make it." Nurse Chrissy added as she walked out of the room. Chuks continued to stare at Pam. "Who is Antoine? You don't have a brother named Antoine, Pam." Chuks responded firmly. Pam came up with something quickly. "Antoine's my therapist, Chuks," Pam replied. "Wow! A therapist needs a therapist. Come on, Pam. Eberechukwu ezi na ulo!" Chuks exclaimed. His voice and accent were becoming more distinct by the second. "You come home at odd hours of the night, all types of different women call on your cell phone, and you don't have time for Nneka. Should I say more?" Pam replied. "You know that I am busy trying to provide a happy life for my family. I am moving up in my career. I am in contact with different people who happen to be co-workers and other individuals of higher ranking who happen to be women. OK, forget that. When were you going to tell me that you were pregnant? You knew I wasn't ready for that now, Pam." Chuks said again, looking disappointed. "That's why I had to get a therapist," Pam snapped angrily. Pam suddenly realized that Chuks didn't want another child yet. Pam glared into Chuks eyes and sadly looked away from him. "Did I lose the baby, Chuks? Did I?" Pam questioned Chuks. "Yeah, we lost the baby. You were bleeding a lot. The doctor couldn't save the baby. It was a boy," Chuks said as he mellowed down. Water began to flow from Pam's eyes as if the tears were dropping from a waterfall. She could not stop herself from crying. At first, Chuks was reluctant to hold Pam. He was hurt and angry. "A baby," Chuks thought. "It would have been our son, my son." Tears began to flow from Chuks eyes. Pam thought, "Is this real or just a dream? A bad dream? I just don't know anymore." Suddenly, Chuks reached out to Pam as they both were grieving together. There was so much hurt and betrayal in the air. How could they ever trust each other again?

Chapter 11

A Blast from the Past

Pam was cooking breakfast for Nneka and her husband. "Baby, please don't overdo it." Chuks pleaded with Pam. He didn't want her to over-exhaust herself after the incident. He would not forgive himself. "Hey babe, don't worry about me. I'll pick up something to eat before I get to the office." Chuks rushes over to kiss his wife on the cheek. "I love you too, honey!" Pam exclaimed. "Mommy, why does Daddy have to go?" Nneka asked her mother as her father ran off... "Your dad has to make money for us. Otherwise, how will you go to Boblo Island without money?" Pam replied. "Oh, ok, mommy, I get it." Nneka looked up, smiling at her mother. Suddenly, Pam's cell phone rings. "Hello," Pam answered. "Hello Pam, it's Velvet," Velvet replied nervously. "How are you?" "I am fine. I am just curious about the nature of this call, especially since it has been over 15 years since we last spoke to each other. I hope all is well." Pam commented. "Pam, all is well. I know that we haven't spoken to each other in years, but I was just thinking about you and your family. How's Chuks?" Velvet asked curiously. "Chuks and Nneka are doing fine. Nneka is our daughter. She's five years old right now. She'll be soon turning six years old in February." Pam continued, "How are you and your family?" "We are all fine. You know I have a fifteen-year-old son. His name is Nicholas. He has grown. He's handsome, like his dad. However, his dad doesn't spend much time with him." Velvet elaborated. "His father is in and out of his life." "Girl, Chuks rushes in and out like he's some type of superhero or something.

Nneka barely sees her father, either." Pam retorted. "What a pattern Chuks had." Both women shared a laugh together that they have not had in a long time. Although Velvet wanted Chuks, she did indeed miss her friendship with Pam. After all, Pam was like a sister that she never had. How on earth could she have ever participated in this love triangle?

"Look, Pam, I need to talk to you about some things. You are like a sister to me. We need to reminisce about the old days. I am in Detroit for the weekend. Why don't we meet at MaMa Bells cafe' for some coffee? You know, talk about the good old days and such. We really need to talk, Pamela Mae." Velvet emphasized. "Oooh, child, no one has called me Pamela Mae in years. You really need to talk," Pam replied. "Yeah, you are the only one that I can talk to. My mother and father have not spoken to me in years. Daddy's company has been in trouble for quite some time. I can't rely on them for any assistance. I've been working two jobs to pay bills and support my son. I just need an outlet and some time to relax." Velvet explains. In Velvet's mind, it was an opportunity to get all her dirty baggage off her chest and to come clean about her relationship with Chuks.

"When do you want to meet with me, Velvet?" Pam asked. "I can make arrangements with Chuks to keep Nneka while I am out. What time do you want to meet at MaMa Bells Cafe?" "How about 1 pm? I wish I could meet Nneka. She sounds amazing.." Velvet commented. "She is amazing, just like her daddy. She is as beautiful as she is smart. A double deuce, I love my family." Pam replied. Something pierced Velvet in the heart. She realized that Chuks had used her body for years and she may never have the life she dreamed about. Her best friend was living the life she desired. "It should have been me. I should have been his wife." Velvet thought. She envied her best friend. She felt betrayed by Chuks. "And now, Chuks, I am going to put an end to your fairy tale marriage. It's time for revenge," Velvet thought as she laughed about what she had done...

Chapter 12

The Big Pay Back

Pam and Velvet arrived at MaMa Bells Cafe' around the same time. The two women were smiling at each other from ear to ear. They embraced each other as they sat down to discuss how well each other was doing. "Girl, I can't remember a time when MaMa Bells 'coffee didn't hit the spot just right. Did you tell Chuks that you were meeting me here? Velvet asked intensely. "No. We have been having problems. I told him that I was going to my therapist. I needed an outlet, you know." Pam said. "Wow! What a way to start the festivities," Velvet thought. The women went on to discuss their lives and the children. "Velvet, you said Nick, oh I mean, Nicholas is fifteen years old. I'm surprised Roberto doesn't spend time with him like that. I thought Roberto would have been a great father to your son and an excellent provider for you. What's up with him? Why does he have so much animosity towards you?" Pam replied. "I don't know, Pam. Men can be very unpredictable. Honestly, I don't want no man hanging round me and hounding me about my whereabouts. As far as I am concerned, I go out, sex them up and lose their number. I don't want to introduce anyone that I am not serious about to Nicholas because he worries about me. He doesn't feel that I should be alone. That's just the path I chose." Velvet confided. "Velvet, I admire you. You got balls. The type I only wish I had. I am so tired of Chuk's late-night workdays, all the co-workers who call him, you know, his undercover female entourage, and all the drama that goes along with it. Yeah, he's a great provider and an extremely good father. The lovemaking is sensational, but........................ I had a miscarriage worrying about that man and his problems. The therapist is not a therapist at all. I met him at the grocery store one day. He was very nice to me when I was pregnant. He was easy to talk to. I dare not air my dirty laundry, but it just felt nice to have someone to talk to." Pam said as she looked away. "Damn, Pam, that bad, huh," Velvet exclaimed while feeling sorry for her friend. Pam began crying. "All I ever wanted was to make him happy and to make my family work. I adore my family. But I am sick of the stipulations, the drama, and most of all, the betrayal coming from him. I can't keep taking this crap." Pam replied. "I clean up; there are little letters, his shirt collars stained with hints of lipstick or perfume on them, which he thinks he is hiding from me. A picture of an adorable little boy that is so handsome that I swear he could pass for his twin. You know, I lost my baby boy! I am so sick of it, and I am drained." Pam cried out. Velvet felt guilty and sorry for Pam at the same time. She didn't want to add on to the betrayal and hurt. However, Pam deserves to know the truth. It's not about Chuks anymore. Pam has got to make some tough decisions.

"Listen, Pam. I have a confession to make. You got to listen to what I am telling you, ok?" "Ok," Pam replied strangely. "One month prior to your wedding day, Roberto and I had a heated argument. I guess you could say we had broken up for the umpteenth time. We broke up countless times. Roberto and I had a passionate yet tumultuous relationship. You see, Roberto loved me, but he wanted to control me. Chuks saw how distraught I was. I was walking home from work that night. Chuks had a late-night internship with a couple of fellas from his class. We walked home together, talking about you and Roberto. We both expressed how much we were in love with you and Roberto. Chuks said you were exactly his type. You were the real deal. He knew he was in love with you. However, when Chuks walked me upstairs to the apartment, my eyes locked into his eyes. One kiss led to another. The kisses were harder and more intense. We held each other tight. Chuks ended up spending the night with me. You were at Tisha's house completing your undergraduate project. Pam, the affair didn't stop. I became pregnant with Nicholas. He is Chuk's son. I am also one of his mistresses." Velvet confessed, looking away from Pam. The look on Pam's face was as if she was going to explode. If she had daggers, she would have stabbed her right where she was sitting. "Bitch, how could you do this to me. My family......... I knew you were a whore, but I didn't believe you would take it there! All this time, I thought you were looking out for me; you were betraying me. You just couldn't be happy for me, could you?" Pam yelled. "Pam, you knew the truth. You just weren't sure who the people involved were. The evidence of Chuks with other women was staring you right in your face. He chose you, Pam! He chose you!" Velvet yelled back at Pam. "And you just used your opportunity to throw your pussy at him, huh? This hurts like hell." Pam cried. "Remember, Pam, it takes two. What are you doing, Pamela Mae?" Velvet exclaimed. Pam took the second cup of hot coffee that she was sipping and tossed it on Velvet's maxi dress. "Thank you for the coffee; it matches your black, hateful soul," Pam shouted as she walked away from the table. "You will thank me later, Pamela Mae." Velvet shouted back "Oooooh, that bitch! The nerve of her." Velvet thought to herself.

Chapter 13

The Argument

"Chukwuka Okafor! I want to talk to you right now!" Pam shouted as she opened the door.

"What's the matter, baby? What has you so angry?" Chuks replied reassuringly.

"Mommy, what's wrong with you? Daddy and I are playing with my dolls. Can we play some more, Daddy?"

"No! Nneka, your father and I have some unfinished business to discuss. Go upstairs to your room now, Nneka," Pam commanded.

"Ahhhh. Mommy, you're no fun. Good night, Daddy," Nneka told her father as she kissed his cheek and ran upstairs to her bedroom.

Chuks approached Pam as if he was going to hug her, but Pam stepped aside.

"Chukwuka, when was the last time you spoke to Velvet?" Pam asked.

"I don't know, Pam. It's been a minute. Why do you ask?" Chuks questioned.

"You should know. She's your mistress and your baby mama. How could you? Right before our wedding day. He's fifteen years old, turning sixteen. Your son. You know, the picture of the boy in your drawer. It all makes sense now. Sandra, Velvet, and God knows whoever else. Is this what you call love? Am I just your convenience so you can have me blinded to your sensual activities? Humiliate me. Convenience, child support, what? Explain it to me now!" Pam demanded.

"I didn't want to hurt you, Pam. I love you. You are the one for me," Chuks said as he looked into her sad brown eyes.

"How about Sandra? Can you explain that? You knew she was my enemy and that she didn't like me. You were sexing up my enemies. Velvet, what about her? Huh?" Pam demanded. She was not there for the foolishness.

"Look, Pam. I know things don't look good, but I do love you. My family in Nigeria adores you and Nneka. They ask me every day when we will come to Nigeria. My mom dreams of the day we will come to see her," Chuks stated.

"BULLSHIT! Let me say THAT again. BULLSHIT! What does that have to do with us right now? I am talking about the here and now," Pam said as she stared at Chuks, getting more and more annoyed.

"Baby, I promise that I will be a good man to you; just don't leave me," Chuks begged.

"Umph, what nerve! Good night, Chuks! You can sleep on the sofa tonight," Pam responded.

Pam went upstairs to her bedroom. She was angry, hurt, and betrayed. She didn't want Nneka to hear her crying, so she buried her head in a pillow and sobbed silently. Then, she came up with an idea. Immediately, she called her sister, Denise.

"Hello, Denise, it's Pam. Listen, I need you to tell Nathan that I need him to send me money so Nneka and I can travel back to Georgia on the bus," Pam said calmly.

"Why, Pam? You and Chuks seem to be getting along with each other well," Denise replied, with some suspicion in her voice.

"Denise, just do what I am asking you to do and trust me. I know what I am doing. I want you to catch the bus up here as if you are visiting us. Bring the money that Nathan will send. While Chuks is at work, we will take everything that we can load up and put the rest in storage until I can return to get the rest of my belongings. We will clean the house. You can help Nneka and me go back to Georgia."

"That's pretty deep, Pam. Ok, I will help you with one condition. I want you to leave me out of your business once you get to Georgia. You know Chuks can be unpredictable at times," Denise replied.

"Just say sneaky, ok. It's a deal," Pam agreed.

Chapter 14

Georgia Sweet Home

Pam, Denise, and Nneka loaded up into Nathan's luxury SUV after visiting their parents.

"Is Tiffany looking forward to our arrival at your home, Nathan?" Pam asked.

"To be honest, no, she isn't," Nathan replied honestly.

"Look, Nathan, I didn't mean to be at odds with your wife. Denise and I need a place to stay until I can get things figured out and back on my feet. That's all. Nneka is driving me crazy about her father. 'Daddy this, Daddy that. I want my Daddy.' Maybe I should have stayed with him... She would have still had her family," Pam replied.

"Look, Pamela Mae, we make some tough choices. You had to make this choice for both your emotional and mental health. You have endured so much, Big Sis. I don't see how you made it, but you did. You are a survivor," Nathan replied. "I never really liked the guy anyway. Gave me a strange vibe whenever he came around. I accepted him as family because of you, Big Sis."

"Nathan, you mean to tell me you didn't like Chuks? The guy you were trying to convince to come to Georgia just to hang out and hunt?" Denise asked with a puzzled look.

"Big mouth. That was only to find out his intentions with Pam and to get to know him better. You know, get some men folk together to sit around and talk over several cans of beer and moonshine. It was to size him up. Besides, coming home to Georgia is just what you gals need anyway. Nneka needs to get to know her American people," Nathan said assuredly.

Nathan and his relatives finally arrived home. Nathan's house was immaculate—not bad for a country lawyer from Georgia. It was hidden away in a secluded, wooded area outside the sprawling city of Greensboro, Georgia. Nathan's home had five bedrooms, a guest room, five bathrooms, a large kitchen, a living room, and a garage that fit four vehicles, along with an enormous backyard. However, something was off.

"Whose car is in the yard?" Pam asked.

"I don't know, Pam. I haven't seen that car around here before," Nathan replied. *Who would dare have the balls to come here? Is Tiffany up to something?* Nathan thought.

As everyone went into the house, there was a surprise sitting on the living room sofa. Tiffany had a smirk a mile wide as she reveled in the intense family drama. She couldn't help but remain cordial for Nathan's sake.

"Chuks! What are you doing here? How did you know?" Pam demanded.

"It's a little hot in here," Pam replied as she fainted to the floor.

"Daddy, I miss you!" Nneka exclaimed as she ran over to her father. Denise was trying to get Pam up off the floor as she greeted Chuks.

"Uh, hi, Chuks. How are you?" Denise asked.

"I'm fine now that I have located my family," Chuks smirked. Tiffany was enjoying every minute of this.

"Would anyone like a drink? Wine, gin, vodka, Hennessy, a fan perhaps?" she asked.

"Gin and OJ for me," Chuks answered, enjoying every moment of the tension. "Hey, Nathan, since I'm here with my family, I am ready for that hunting excursion you promised me," Chuks replied as he smiled deviously at the crowd.

It was silent. You could hear a pin drop. Everyone sat frozen in their seats, in suspense.

TO BE CONTINUED

Made in the USA
Columbia, SC
20 November 2024

47129618R00048